dick bruna

miffy
is
crying

World International

Miffy lay asleep in bed

with Teddy next to her

she thought how warm and friendly

it felt to have him there.

But when the night was over

poor Miffy cried, oh dear,

do you know what had happened?

her teddy was not here.

Oh, what could have become of him

where could her teddy be

she looked in every corner

there's Miffy, you can see.

She went to ask her father –

her mum was out that day –

do you know where my teddy's gone?

Father Bun couldn't say.

She went and asked her little friends

out playing in the grass

but there was not a single one

who knew where teddy was.

She went to ask her grandma

and grandpa too, who said,

although I haven't left the house

I haven't seen your ted.

And then she asked her auntie

who lived up on the hill

but she had not seen anything –

her tears began to spill.

So Miffy went back home again

not knowing what to do

oh, how hard poor Miffy cried

she loved her teddy too.

But when the day was over –

look, you can see her here –

and Miffy was in bed again

her feet felt something near.

She crept beneath the blankets, and

do you know what she found?

a furry something with two arms

its shape was nice and round.

She brought it up beside her

look, look, it's nearly there

a yellow something, with a head,

can it be Miffy's bear?

Here is my bear, cried Miffy

here is my bear, for sure

hurrah, I've found my teddy –

and Miffy cried no more.

miffy's library

"nijntje huilt"
Original text Dick Bruna 1991 © copyright Mercis Publishing BV.
Illustrations Dick Bruna © copyright Mercis BV 1991.
Published in Great Britain in 1997 by World International Ltd.,
Deanway Technology Centre, Wilmslow Road, Handforth, Cheshire SK9 3FB.
Original English translation © copyright Patricia Crampton 1996.
The moral right of the author has been asserted.
Publication licensed by Mercis Publishing BV, Amsterdam.
Printed by Sebald Sachsendruck Plauen, Germany. All rights reserved.
ISBN 0-7498-2981-8